Haunted Castle Tour

Spooky!

At Weasel Towers tonight...

Watch out!
Weasel in ghost costume about!

HUNGRY CROCS IN THE MOAT

£20

FAT CAT

Wants new home/owner, preferably with large swimming pool.
Only eats caviar from a silver dish.
Call Mr Tibbles: 06571-287

─MISSING─

4 large, dangerous crocodiles, stolen from the safari park 2 weeks ago. If found do not panic – call Stan's Safari Park.

WEASEL'S AUTOS

W

USED CARS

Every car is guaranteed to break down as soon as you leave my garage!

MAKE A FORTUNE

from

GETTING RICH T... @eas... W...

EAT AT WEASEL BURGER

Unhealthy food, terrible service!

COUPON

1 for 2

For Hairy Toes,
Furry Paws
and Arthur

This book belongs to:

Sneaky Weasel ESQ

and

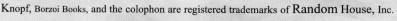

THIS IS A BORZOI BOOK PUBLISHED BY ALFRED A. KNOPF

Copyright © 2008 by Hannah Shaw

All rights reserved. Published in the United States by Alfred A. Knopf,
an imprint of Random House Children's Books,
a division of Random House, Inc., New York.

Originally published in Great Britain in 2008 by Jonathan Cape, an imprint of Random House Children's Books.

Knopf, Borzoi Books, and the colophon are registered trademarks of Random House, Inc.

Visit us on the Web! www.randomhouse.com/kids

Educators and librarians, for a variety of teaching tools,
visit us at www.randomhouse.com/teachers

Library of Congress Cataloging-in-Publication Data is available on request.

ISBN 978-0-375-85625-9 (trade) ISBN 978-0-375-95625-6 (lib. bdg.)

The illustrations in this book were created using a combination of pen and ink, printmaking techniques, and Photoshop.

MANUFACTURED IN MALAYSIA
February 2009

10 9 8 7 6 5 4 3 2 1

First American Edition

Random House Children's Books supports the First Amendment and celebrates the right to read.

Sneaky Weasel

Hannah Shaw

ALFRED A. KNOPF ✣ NEW YORK

Weasel was sneaky.

He was a bully and a cheat
– a nasty, measly Weasel.

His mean schemes and cunning tricks
had made him richer than
you can possibly imagine.

IT'S GOOD TO BE SNEAKY!

WEASEL
BANK
GIVE ME YOUR MONEY

JOKE SHOP

WEAS
AUT

Sneaky
Weasel INC.

One day Weasel decided to throw a party to boast about his incredible castle, fast car and huge swimming pool.

He sent off invitations to everyone he could think of.

On *the day* of the party
Weasel dressed in his finest clothes
and admired himself in the mirror.

"Don't I look handsome?"
he asked his reflection.

Then Weasel waited expectantly for his guests to arrive.

He waited...

and Waited...

But no one came.

Being rich and powerful isn't much fun when there's no one to impress.

"Why would anyone not want to come to my party?" sulked Weasel.

"I will visit them all and demand an explanation."

First, Weasel went to see Rabbit. He banged on the door.
When Rabbit saw Weasel, he started *shaking*.
"What's the matter with **you**?" Said Weasel crossly.
"And why didn't you come to **my** party?"

Next, Weasel went to see Rat in his laboratory. "Why didn't you come to my party?" he snapped.

Rat gulped nervously. He wanted to run and hide!
"B-because you ruined my v-very
important scientific experiment,"
he stammered.

"I was just trying to help,"
lied Weasel.

Off Weasel went to visit Hedgehog,
but on the way he met Hedgehog's mum.
"Hedgehog isn't *very* well," she said.

"He's been scratching for days and days and he just can't stop."

"Ah," said Weasel, feeling a bit itchy himself.

Weasel was starting to feel quite *guilty*,
so he *crept* past Shrew's house.

"Not so *fast*," said a little voice.

"It was a joke," protested Weasel.
"My cat only likes caviar,
    he wouldn't eat you."

"Well it wasn't funny," squeaked Shrew.

"Nobody came to your party because you're mean and nasty and a bad friend. And you never ever say sorry!"

Weasel went *home* feeling *measly*.
He had been a *horrible bully*.

"I *must find* a way to be a *good* friend,"
he thought desperately,

"but h*ow*?"

Weasel paced **round** and **round** all night,
trying to think of good ideas.
This wasn't *easy* because
most of *his* thoughts were *wickedly* sneaky,
but by morning he had a pla*n* . . .

"What I need to do," said Weasel,

"is put right everything I've done wrong."

So that is exactly what he did.

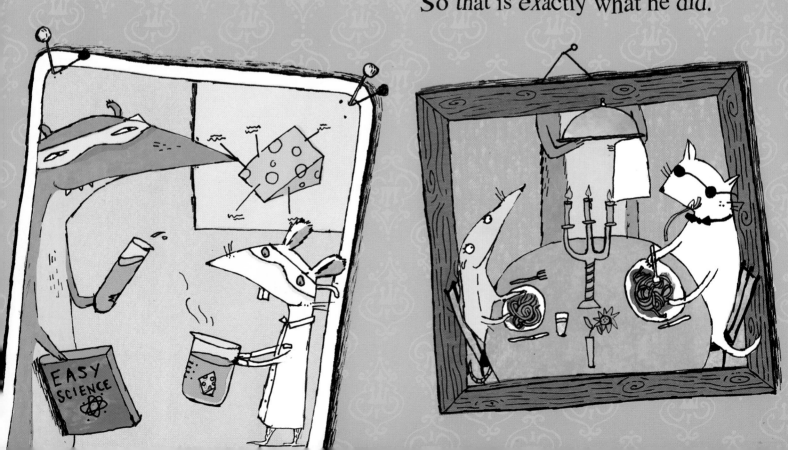

Everyone was pleased that Weasel was making *such* an effort.

"But there is still one thing we *have*n't heard you say," said Shrew.

Weasel thought long and hard. After a while, he began to mumble,

"I'm *so* . . . *so* important! No . . . I'm *su* . . . super sneaky?"

The other animals began to laugh.

"I've got it!" cried Weasel.

"I'm Sorry!"

"Hurray!" they all cheered.

Weasel decided to throw a party
to celebrate being good at being good.

invitation

Dear friends,

Please come to my party.
There will be jelly, cake and
ice cream and I will be on my
best behavior.

Yours sincerelyish,

Weasel

P.S. Don't worry,
the crocodiles in the
moat have been sent
back to the safari park.

And *I*'d like to say that Weasel *finally* learned
the error of his ways and stopped being sneaky altogether.

But *sometimes* he just couldn't help himself . . .